STRIKE OUT!

ASPHODEL PUBLIC LIBRARY
WESTWOOD, ONT. KOL 3B0

Tristan Howard

A
LITTLE **APPLE**
PAPERBACK

W9-ASY-294

SCHOLASTIC INC.
New York Toronto London Auckland Sydney

For Jonathan Howard

If you purchased this book without a cover, you should be aware that this book is stolen property. It was reported as "unsold and destroyed" to the publisher, and neither the author nor the publisher has received any payment for this "stripped book."

No part of this publication may be reproduced in whole or in part, or stored in a retrieval system, or transmitted in any form or by any means, electronic, mechanical, photocopying, recording, or otherwise, without written permission of the publisher. For information regarding permission, write to Scholastic Inc., 555 Broadway, New York, NY 10012.

ISBN 0-590-56923-6

Copyright © 1996 by Daniel Weiss Associates, Inc. Conceived by Ed Monagle, Michael Pollack, and Daniel Weiss. Grateful acknowledgment to Elise Howard. All rights reserved. Published by Scholastic Inc. APPLE PAPERBACKS and the APPLE PAPERBACKS logo ® are registered trademarks of Scholastic Inc. Cover art copyright © 1996 by Daniel Weiss Associates, Inc. Interior illustrations by Marcy Ramsey.

Produced by Daniel Weiss Associates, Inc.
33 West 17th Street, New York, NY 10011

12 11 10 9 8 7 6 5 4 3 2 1   6 7 8 9/9 0 1/0

Printed in the U.S.A.   40

First Scholastic printing, April 1996

David "Too Tall" Henry walked to the plate. He was the best—and biggest—player in the entire Maplewood Township Baseball League.

"Catherine! Adam! Josh!" our manager, Mr. Barnett, called toward the outfield. "Take three giant steps back!"

"Mother, may I?" shouted Adam.

"Yes, you may," Josh answered in a high, squeaky voice.

Too Tall stood at home plate and pounded the end of the bat into the dust. Then he lifted his hand to his batting helmet and touched the bill one, two, three times.

At last Too Tall was ready. He lifted the bat to swing.

Whack! I could hear the explosion all the way out in center field, even three steps back.

"Oooh!" said the crowd. *"Ahhh!"*

"Don't throw the bat, honey!" That was Too Tall's mother.

The ball rose through the air, going up, up, up, and out, out, out, straight to center field.

I lifted my glove and went back for the catch. "I got it! I got it!" I yelled. The ball was high, but I stretched as tall as I could and leaped to meet it.

Plonk. I had it. I, Catherine "Shorty" Antler, had snagged one from Too Tall Henry and gotten him out!

The crowd went wild.

Two more Orioles were still running the bases. I threw the ball to second base, where my best friend, Amy Powell, was waiting. She caught the ball and tagged the runner "out." Then she whirled around to fire the ball to our other best friend, Michael Grassi, at third base.

Amy's throw was a little wild, but Michael jumped for it. He came down on the base with the ball in his glove and tagged that runner, too. Triple play! With only two Orioles left to bat, they couldn't catch us now. The Rangers had beaten the best team in the league!

As I was racing to give Michael and Amy a high five, I heard someone calling me. "Catherine, you're up!"

How could I be up? I was still playing center field.

Then the field began to shake all around me. The voice grew louder. "Get up!" it said. "Get up!"

Oh, no, I thought, rubbing my closed eyes as the field melted away.

Opening them, I looked around.

My mom sat on the edge of my bed, gently jiggling my shoulder. My glove hung from the bedpost.

It had all been a dream.

I knew why I had dreamed that great game, though. The baseball season was about to begin for real. Soon Amy, Michael, and I—the dream team—would be together again.

It was our second year in the Maplewood Township Baseball League. Michael and I were already best friends before we started playing. We met Amy playing for the Rangers, but we stayed friends all summer. Now that we were in third grade, we couldn't wait to play together again.

It was the day the league would send out all the letters telling us who else would be on the Rangers for the year.

We talked about it that day at recess, when I told Michael and Amy about my dream.

"Getting a triple play against Too Tall would be cool," Michael said. "But it would be cooler if Too Tall was on our team."

"Yuck!" said Amy. "I don't care if he *is* the best player. He never combs his hair, he's always got food on his shirt, and he makes rude noises!"

"You mean like this?" Michael asked, and he pressed his hand against his mouth and blew.

"Gross, Michael!" Amy complained, but she looked as if she might laugh.

"Mr. Grassi . . ." That was Mr. Becker's warning voice. Poor Michael. The playground monitor always caught him at just the wrong time.

That afternoon the phone was ringing as I came into the house.

"I got it! I got it!" I yelled.

Behind me, my mom was shouting, "Take off your coat! No call is that important!"

My mom just didn't understand about baseball. When my parents got divorced and my dad moved to another state, she made up her mind that I would not miss out on anything kids with two parents got to do. So when I said I wanted to join baseball, she said okay right away.

She came to all my games if she could, and cheered whenever she thought she should. But my mom's idea of a fun sport was pulling weeds out of her garden. You couldn't talk to her about things like strategy or batting practice or whether aluminum bats were better than wooden ones.

She would try to listen, but she would always get this funny look in her eyes. Even though her mouth was saying, "Uh-huh," her brain was thinking, *Should I plant pansies or petunias this year?*

It was Amy on the phone. "Did you open it?" she asked.

"Not yet. I—"

"You gotta open it!"

"Wait a sec," I said. "I just got home." I turned to the table where my mom usually put the mail, but she was already handing me the envelope.

I ripped it open, looked at the letter, and grinned. "All right!" I shouted. "Rangers rule!"

Amy didn't say anything.

"Are you there?" I asked. "Amy?"

"Rangers rule," she said quietly. "But this year I'm on the Orioles."

This was *truly* terrible news.

"Well, that stinks." It was the only thing I could think of to say. "Michael and I will really miss you."

"Not as much as I'll miss you guys," Amy said.

After Amy and I said good-bye, I wanted to call Michael right away, but he was in

Extended Day at school because his mom and dad both worked in the city. So I couldn't call him until six o'clock.

I did my homework and tried to think of ways to cheer up poor Amy.

At six o'clock exactly I called Michael. His phone was busy. I tried again five minutes later, and his mom told me that he had gone to Amy's house. Strange.

Just as I was about to go to Amy's house, the doorbell rang. It was Amy and Michael. Amy didn't look as if she felt so bad anymore, but Michael hadn't looked so awful since the day his mom accidentally dropped the sofa on his pet mouse, Whiskers.

"Guess what!" Amy was bouncing back and forth from one foot to the other.

"Cut it out, Amy," Michael warned her.

"What?" I asked. "You guys, what's going on?"

"I'm not on the Rangers, either," Michael said.

"Oh, no!" I wailed. "How could they split us up?"

Just then the phone rang, but this time I let my mom answer it.

"Catherine," Michael said, "they didn't exactly split us up. I'm on the Orioles, too."

Amy and Michael together on the best team in the league? Me, all alone, on the Rangers, the absolute worst of the worst without Amy and Michael? My day, which had started out so perfectly with an amazing triple play, could not have gotten any more horrible—or so I thought.

My mom came back into the room with a big smile on her face. "Guess what!" she said.

I groaned. "I can't take any more guessing," I told her.

"That was your league director, Mr. Buturla. Unfortunately, Mr. Barnett has been transferred to a job in another state. He can't manage the Rangers this year."

I was getting a funny feeling in my stomach, and it was spreading fast to my arms and legs.

"So," Mom said, "Mr. Buturla asked me to take the job, and I said yes. Isn't that wonderful? Aren't we going to have fun?" My mom, who didn't know the difference between a shortstop and a dugout, was going to manage my baseball team.

I groaned again, and Michael poked me with his elbow.

Why couldn't somebody wake me up from *this* dream?

Chapter 2

It was Saturday, the first day of practice, and we had started with batting.

"Brenda Bailey?" Mom called out, looking down at her clipboard. "Brenda?"

At last Brenda waved two gooey fingers in the air. With her other hand she was trying to stuff an empty candy wrapper into her pocket, which wasn't easy, since her shorts were a little on the tight side. Her mouth was busy chewing as she walked to the plate.

Mom had sent us all to the field, and now she was calling people to come hit. The good news was that it wasn't any worse than I had expected. The bad news was that I had expected the worst.

A few kids were back from the previous year. Lucy Marcus, Adam Fingerhut, Julie Zimmer, Matt Carter, and Josh Ramos had all been on the Rangers in second grade. Me, too. Our only new third-grader was from the Orioles, a kid named Alex Slavik. So far he didn't seem like a fair trade for Amy and Michael. Alex *was* smart. He was always winning prizes at school and was the kind of kid who got to leave school on some days to take special advanced classes. But he was very skinny and pale, as if he spent a lot of time studying for those special classes. And he had enormous feet— the kind that looked perfect for tripping over on the way to first base.

We had four new second-graders: Brenda, a new girl in school named Yin Wong from China, Mitchell Rubin, and Danny West.

Adam had batted first. His first hit was good, but it went straight to Julie in center field. Lucky for Adam, Julie was wearing her new pink sweatshirt, which her mom had bought especially for practice. Julie didn't want to mess it up with mud or grease or grass stains. She was busy dusting off invisible dirt particles when the ball fell in front of her. Josh Ramos ran to scoop it up, but it was too late. Adam was safe at home.

After Adam, Yin went. She was okay, but so slow that first base was a long trip. She'd be an easy out every time.

I had hopes for Danny West. He was pretty scrawny and didn't like to sit still much, but he could talk all about major-league baseball. He also had brand-new metal cleats (the rest of us wore sneakers), his own bat, a fancy new glove, and a catcher's mitt, too. And he was chewing the biggest, fattest wad of grape bubble gum I'd ever seen. Just like a major-league player.

But when he went to bat, he couldn't even get a piece of the ball. It was three swings, three strikes. Maybe the gum had thrown him off balance.

Now it was Brenda's turn. She swung— and missed by a mile.

"Try opening your eyes, honey," Mom suggested.

So Brenda swung again, with her eyes open so wide she reminded me of a poster for a horror movie. She missed again, but I guess the breeze knocked the ball off the plate, and it rolled slowly through the dust behind home plate.

"Matt?" Mom called. Matt was playing catcher. At least he was supposed to be playing catcher. Instead he was squatting down in the dirt, poking something with a twig.

"Look," he said when Mom called him. "A grasshopper."

"Really?" Mom said, bending over. *Oh, no,* I thought. She'd been doing great so far.

But Josh Ramos stomped over from the bench and stood over the ball, which had come to a stop a couple of feet behind the plate. "Look, Carter!" he bellowed. "A ball!" Josh was still steamed about Adam's home run. It did seem to snap Mom and Matt out of it, though.

"All right, Brenda. One more try," Mom said after the ball was back on the plate. But Brenda just looked at her, frowning, and shook her head.

"Finished for now? Okay, Brenda." Mom smiled, and Brenda went back to right field as Mom scribbled something on her clipboard.

"Hey!" I yelled. "She's not done yet!" That was the first time I'd ever seen anybody just stop after getting only two strikes.

"Yeah!" Josh shouted. "She's not out until she gets three strikes."

"Never mind," Mom said. "She got two strikes today. Maybe she'll get three tomorrow."

Brenda just pulled another little package out of her pocket and began eating gumdrops.

"Me, me!" yelled Danny West, who wanted to bat again.

But Mom chose Lucy Marcus. Lucy picked up the bat, walked to the plate, and hit a line drive. The ball sailed flat and straight across the infield, right to Danny, who stood holding his glove in front of him, waiting for it. He was still standing and waiting when the ball dropped to the ground and streaked right through his legs.

I turned to see how far around the bases Lucy was. But she had never left home plate. She was making faces and clowning for

Matt, who was laughing so hard he had fallen down in the dirt.

Meanwhile the ball rolled through center field, where Alex Slavik had actually caught it, or at least picked it up after it stopped rolling. I signaled to him from my position at first base. If he threw it to me, I could step on the base to get Lucy out.

Alex didn't even see me. He cranked his arm around and around like a windmill and launched the ball toward home plate. Or tried to. He let go just a little too late, and the ball headed like a missile into the ground about ten feet in front of him, where it landed so hard it dug up a little clump of grass.

But it didn't matter. Matt was so busy laughing that even if Alex's throw had been perfect, Matt never would have seen it.

Baseball is a pretty simple game. The runner hits the ball, then runs as far as she can around the bases without getting tagged out. The team in the field can get the runner out three ways. They can catch the ball in the air after she hits it, tag the runner with the ball while she's not safe on a base, or step on the base before the runner gets there.

But as I looked at Lucy and Matt and the ball, which was just lying there, I wondered, *If the runner isn't running, and the fielders aren't fielding, is the runner safe? Or is she out?*

The team looked like it was made up of bits and pieces—weird kids that would never fit anywhere else. Like yucky leftovers in the fridge that no one really wants. In my secret thoughts, the Rangers became "the Leftovers." I wondered if we'd ever become a real team.

One thing I knew for sure: The Rangers were not a *safe* bet to win the Maplewood Township Baseball League championship that year. We weren't even a safe bet to win a game. In fact, we had a lot of work to do if we didn't want to be totally *out* of the competition.

Chapter 3

"You should have been there, Catherine," Michael was saying. "Too Tall was awesome." It was Monday, and we were eating lunch together. The Orioles first practice had been on Saturday, too.

"Yeah," Amy agreed. She nodded so hard I thought her chin would land in her mashed potatoes. "A home run every time. And he's a great fielder, too."

"Plus he's got a great arm," Michael said. "You should have seen him, Catherine."

"So I heard," I said. "Amy, I thought you couldn't stand Too Tall."

"I never said that," Amy protested very seriously. I started to remind her about everything she had said at that same table less than one week before, but I could see that it would be no use. Ever since we'd sat down, Amy and Michael had talked about nothing but how great the Orioles were. Great players, great coach, even great uniforms.

"Did you tell Catherine about your nickname?" Michael asked Amy.

Amy laughed. "Coach Popple says I look just like a major-league player named Lefty Leo Lohman, 'cause he bats left and so do I. So he started calling me Lefty Leo."

That made me start to think of nicknames for the Rangers. Danny "Cleats" West. Julie "Fashion Bug" Zimmer. Brenda "Chubs" Bailey. "Minnesota Twins" for Lucy and Matt. And Alex "Feet" Slavik.

"So, how are the good ol' Rangers?" Michael asked, as if he could read my mind.

I opened my mouth, then shut it. When I opened it again, the strangest words came out. "Oh, we're just great!" I said. "Just great."

"Brenda," Mom said, "that's much, much better."

"Yeah, great," I said, frowning. "That's just great."

It was the second day of Rangers practice, Wednesday evening. Mom had divided us into two teams for a practice game.

Brenda had improved since Saturday, sort of. This time she got three strikes in a row.

Danny West was sulking. He wouldn't play because Mom had told him cleats weren't allowed and he would have to wear regular sneakers like everybody else.

Julie had just painted her fingernails before practice. When it was her turn to bat, she held the bat sort of loosely in her hands, so that she wouldn't smear her nail polish. In a way it worked, because the bat and ball connected with a loud *crack,* and the ball soared through the air toward center field.

There was only one small problem. Julie's grip was so light that the bat went flying after the ball, twirling through the air like a giant, heavy wooden baton. "Duck!" Adam yelled, and Rangers scattered in every direction—including Mitchell, who so far had spent the whole practice sitting down in right field, except when it was his turn to bat. Only Julie kept running around the bases.

Then, just as I was losing hope for the entire season, something funny happened. Yin came to bat again, and slammed the ball out to center field so hard that she had enough time to run to second base.

Then Josh got another hit, but Lucy, who had been showing Yin how to do handstands at second base, stopped long enough to make a catch and get him out.

The Rangers kept playing well. Soon the bases were loaded, with Yin on third, Adam on second, and Mitchell on first. Then Alex came to bat.

BASES LOADED

"All right! Looking good! Butter up! Butter up!" my mom yelled. I was too embarrassed to say anything.

"It's '*batter* up,' Mrs. Antler," Josh informed her.

Even though it was only practice, Alex looked a little nervous. He wiped his palms on his T-shirt, adjusted his batting helmet, and picked up the bat. Then he dropped the bat to adjust his helmet one more time. He picked up the bat again, swung, and missed by a mile.

"C'mon," I cheered. "You can do it! Go, batter!"

Alex swung again and connected! The ball blooped into foul territory behind home plate.

"All right!" Matt yelled. "Way to get a piece of it!"

"Yo, batter!" Adam yelled from second base.

Soon all the Rangers were cheering Alex on. Alex choked up on the bat, gripping it a little bit higher this time, swung, and connected!

The ball flew high in the air before it began to come down. It was headed in the direction of first base. So was Alex. And somehow the ball and Alex managed to meet on the way. The ball fell right on Alex's head. Luckily, it bounced off his batting helmet.

"Alex, honey, are you okay?" Mom called. When Alex nodded, she said, "Good, but I guess you're out, dear."

Meanwhile the ball had bounced directly

from Alex's head to second base—so Mitchell was out, too.

Adam had started running from second base to third, but he had turned around to see if Alex was okay. He began running again, but it was too late. Lucy just picked up the ball and tagged him out.

Alex Slavik had made a triple play—for the wrong side. Not only were the Rangers bad to begin with, but there was a jinx on the team as well. We were doomed.

Chapter 4

That Friday, when Ms. Kellam asked for volunteers to stay in and help her organize the classroom a little bit at recess, I raised my hand. Michael and Amy were surprised, because I was always the first one on the playground, but I needed a break. I was getting really tired of hearing about the *wonderful* Orioles, *wonderful* Coach Popple, and most of all *wonderful* Too Tall Henry.

I was full of energy, and I scrubbed the blackboard, dusted the bookshelves and cubbies, and helped organize the supply cabinet.

Ms. Kellam was busy taking down the winter posters from the bulletin board and putting up new ones for spring when she ran out of thumbtacks. She sent me to Mr. Shockley's room to see if he had some extras.

"I was just going down to the office to take a phone call," Mr. Shockley told me. "But you may look in the arts and crafts box in the coat nook. If I have any, they'll be there."

I was heading over to the coat nook when I heard a commotion on the playground. It was a warm day, and the windows were all open. I went over to see what the fuss was all about.

A big group of kids was clustered together on the basketball court. Amy and Michael were there. So were Adam and Josh and Julie. They were laughing and having a good time, it seemed. But then I could see that they were making fun of someone in the middle—someone who had apparently made a basket for the wrong team. I heard somebody shout, "Wrong way! Wrong way! Play for us another day!" It was the familiar voice of Too Tall Henry.

Then the crowd broke up and began playing again—all except for one kid. From the windows, I could see Alex Slavik walk away,

25

ASPHODEL PUBLIC LIBRARY
WESTWOOD, ONT. K0L 3B0

head down, from the basketball court. He really was a jinx.

I turned around and went back to the coat nook to look for the thumbtacks. It wasn't easy. It was dark in there, and Mr. Shockley's supplies were a big mess. I had to sort through bottles of glue, rolls of tape, and tubes of glitter, and still had not found any thumbtacks when the classroom door opened.

I knew right away it was not Mr. Shockley. It was a kid, a kid who was starting to cry. I froze in the coat nook. Luckily, Mr. Shockley came in a minute later.

"Alex," he said. "What's the problem, my man?"

"Basketball," Alex told him. "I stink, so they kicked me out of the game."

"Well, you may not be great at basketball," Mr. Shockley said, "but think of everything you can do better than most people, like math and science and reading."

"But I like sports," Alex said. "I want to be good at sports. I have a good time until it's my turn, then I just mess everything up and make everybody mad."

Mr. Shockley didn't say anything for a

while. Then he said, "C'mon. Let's go see if the cafeteria ladies have any of those big chocolate chip cookies left."

I waited until I heard the door click shut behind them. Then I found the thumbtacks and got back to Ms. Kellam's room as fast as I could.

It rained all night Friday. On Saturday morning the sky was still dark and gray, and the field where the Rangers practiced was soggy. It was a sleepy day, and everybody seemed to be having trouble concentrating. One thing caught my attention right away, though: Alex had not come to practice.

I couldn't exactly blame him. Everybody was talking about what had happened at school the day before. And even though I felt sorry for him, I couldn't help thinking, *If he really is a jinx, aren't the Rangers better off without him?*

"Has anybody heard from Alex this morning?" Mom asked.

"You mean Wrong Way?" Josh whispered to Adam, and they both snickered behind their hands.

"Maybe he went to the wrong field," Lucy said.

"Maybe he's going to show up *tomorrow*," said Matt.

"Hey! Maybe he's been playing for the wrong team all along," said Julie. "Maybe he just found out he's really on the Cardinals." A couple of people cheered when Julie said that. I didn't say anything.

But a few minutes later a car pulled up. Alex came onto the field, and I heard his mom explaining to mine, "My little ones both came down with the chicken pox this morning, just when my husband is away on business. I tried to talk Alex into staying home, but he wouldn't miss practice for the world. Finally I found a neighbor to sit with Annetta and John while I brought him over."

"Here, honey!" she called to Alex. "Don't forget your sweatshirt."

"Yeah," muttered Josh. "Just don't put it on inside out."

Alex didn't hear that comment. And I was

29

pretty sure Josh and the others just wanted to be funny, not mean.

We practiced hitting for a while, then we concentrated on fielding. Mom assigned us each to different positions, then tried hitting the ball to us so that everyone could see where they played best. It was a good idea, except for two problems. Mom's aim wasn't very good, although that kept us all on our toes. And for most of the Rangers, the question was not where they were best. The question was where they were a little less terrible—meaning where they might have a small chance of catching the ball once in a while. Like I said, it was a good *idea*.

We ended with another practice game. We didn't have enough people for two real teams, but Mom put most people in the field, with a few up at bat, and had us trade off to give everybody a turn.

The bases were loaded, with Matt on third, Yin on second, and Julie on first, when I stepped up to the plate. Mr. Buturla had stopped by to speak with Mom, and they started walking over to the parking lot. "I'll only be a moment. Keep playing," Mom said.

I was just choking up and planting my feet firmly on the muddy ground when a loud, familiar shout interrupted my concentration.

"Yo, Anteater! Give it up!" It was Too Tall Henry and a few other Orioles, including Amy and Michael, who waved at me. They had been practicing on another field at the park. Their practice must have let out early.

"*Woooo!*" Too Tall yelled. "*Whoooaaa!*" He threw in a couple of other gross noises, too. He sounded ridiculous, but he was trying to distract me, and it was working. But he was making me angry, too. I wasn't going to let Too Tall ruin my game.

NO BATTER . . . NO BATTER

I blocked out the noise, pulled my bat back, and swung it hard. I felt the wooden bat connect with the ball, which lifted high into the air.

As I was running around the bases I heard a voice shout, "I got it!" That was Alex. Then another voice, Josh's, shouted, "*I got it!*" Then came the crash. By the time I got to first base, Josh and Alex were sprawled side by side on their backs on the wet grass of center field. Neither one of them had the ball.

"Huh huh huh," Too Tall laughed. "Did you know Alex is our secret weapon? All we have to do is send him to play for another team."

"Why don't you get lost, David Henry?" I shouted. I couldn't believe my eyes when I saw Too Tall and the rest of the Orioles scatter. Then I turned around to see my mom and Mr. Buturla heading across the field.

Neither Josh nor Alex was really hurt. They just rubbed their heads for a few seconds, then slowly stood up. Except that when Alex stood up, he began walking across the field, away from practice and toward the parking lot.

"Alex!" Mom called. "Practice isn't over yet!"

Alex turned around. "I know what people say," he said. "Even at school they say I'm a jinx and I stink. They're right. I quit." And he turned around and kept walking.

Nobody did anything for a little while. Then Brenda Bailey ran over to the bench and picked up her jacket. At first I thought

she was going to leave, too. Instead she pulled a large red lollipop from her pocket and went running after Alex. Then Danny took off his glove, tucked it under his arm, and went after her. Soon Yin, then Julie, then Josh and the rest of the team were running across the field and up the hill toward Baker Street. I don't think Brenda had ever run so hard in her life. Even Mitchell Rubin was slowly jogging along at the back of the line.

We caught up with Alex when he had to stop for cars at the street. He looked pretty surprised to see us all there. He rubbed his eyes hard, as if he had been crying. Then Brenda just held the lollipop out to him. It looked kind of old and smashed up, as if she had been carrying it around for a while. But Alex took it, and his frown slowly turned into a small smile.

"Here," Danny said, stepping forward. "Why don't you try my glove for a while?"

"Really?" Alex asked, reaching for it.

"Here," Yin said, lifting a gold chain that had been hidden inside her shirt from around her neck. It had a charm on it that looked like some Chinese writing I had once seen. "From my grandmother when I leave

China for America. Good luck for my hitting!" It was the most I had ever heard Yin say at one time, and she seemed to be concentrating very hard. Everyone laughed, because now we knew why Yin was such a great hitter. Alex let her put it over his head.

Then Adam noticed that Josh was shoving something back into his pocket. "Hey, what are you doing?" he asked.

Josh turned as red as the tulips at the edge of the sidewalk. "Never mind. He doesn't need it," he said.

But Adam wrestled him to the ground and pulled a tattered square of filthy pink fabric from his pocket. "Look, everybody! It's Josh's blankie!" he cried.

Josh looked really, really mad. "Is not!" he yelled. "It's . . . it's a cloth for wiping my hands when I bat."

Uh-oh, I thought. Josh looked ready to kill Adam, and if he did, we'd be down three players: Alex, Adam, and Josh, who would probably be kicked off the team for murder.

But Alex came to the rescue. "Gee, maybe I could use that," he said. "Especially if I eat this lollipop."

Then Julie stepped forward. She didn't have anything to give him, but she took out a tissue and tried to wipe the grass stains and mud off Alex's sleeves and pant legs. Actually, he looked kind of annoyed by that.

But he didn't seem so upset about baseball anymore. And when Mom called us back over to the practice field, he came along with the rest of the crowd, Yin's charm around his neck, Danny's glove on his hand, and Brenda's lollipop and Josh's blankie—I mean cloth—stuffed into his pocket.

The rest of the practice went great—for a Rangers practice, at least. It was as if everyone wanted to help Alex so much that they forgot about their own troubles. Like when Brenda was up. Alex was on third base, Lucy was on second, and Matt was on first. Brenda was the last batter before we traded sides. If she hit the ball, Alex would get to run home. If she missed, he had made it all the way to third base for nothing.

Brenda swung once and missed. She swung again and missed again.

"All right, Brenda. Let's bring him on home," Mom said. Even Mom was getting the hang of things. At first Brenda looked at her as if she were crazy. Then she took her third swing, and everyone cheered when the ball flew off the bat.

Well, maybe not *flew* off the bat. It was more like it rolled off. But it was good enough for Alex to score. All the Rangers cheered again when he came running across home plate.

RUN!! RUN!

Finally practice was over, and parents began to arrive to pick up their kids. "Great practice!" Mom announced as we collected our gear. "Before you go," she went on, "I have an announcement. Wednesday is our first game, as you know. Today I received the schedule, which I have right here."

She took a piece of paper from her pocket and began unfolding it. "So let's meet here Wednesday evening, uniforms on, heads up, attitudes positive, and ready to beat . . ." Everybody was quiet as she looked down at her paper. "The Orioles!"

Mom looked up with a big grin. I think

she expected everyone to cheer and shout at the end of her pep talk. But for a moment nobody said a word. Things had been looking up, all right, but not so far up that we were ready for the Orioles.

Then Yin shouted, "Beat the Orioles!" in a voice that surprised us all.

"Beat the Orioles!" Lucy yelled, and she reached over to give Matt a high five.

Soon everybody was yelling, "Beat the Orioles! Beat the Orioles!" until the crowd broke up and everybody's parents drove them home.

"So," Mom said to me as we headed back to our house, "think we can beat these Orioles on Wednesday?"

She looked so happy. I didn't want to spoil it for her. "Sure we can," I said. But I was really wondering if there was just some way we could keep the game from being a total disaster.

Chapter
6

The Orioles thought they could psych us out on Wednesday. They all wore their team T-shirts to school that day, orange and white with *Orioles* written across the front in black cursive letters and *Maplewood Triple Cinemas,* the name of their team's sponsor, on the back. But the Rangers were ready. We had on our T-shirts, too. Ours were green and white with *Rangers* in big gold letters on the front. The back said *Worms 'n' More Bait Shop.*

All day long, whenever we had a chance, we would give each other high fives and say, "Go, Rangers!" The second-graders looked pretty pleased when we third-graders high-fived them in the halls, even if the teachers did tell us to quiet down.

I was a little worried about going to the cafeteria at lunchtime. Earlier that week, special testing days for the third grade had changed our lunch schedules, so I didn't have to think about it. But now I wondered whether Amy and Michael and I would sit together, as usual, or sit with our teams. Everything seemed different—especially now that we had our uniforms on.

I had to go through the hot-lunch line, and Michael and Amy both brought their lunches. When I came out of the line with my tray, I saw Michael horsing around with Too Tall and some other Orioles at a table.

But then I heard a voice. "Catherine! Catherine Antler!" Amy was trying to catch me before I sat down, and I was happy to see her.

"How come you're not sitting with the Orioles?" I asked.

Amy looked down at her sandwich and wrinkled her nose. At first I thought she was going to say that the Orioles had kicked her out of their table because her tuna fish smelled. Her mom always packed very nutritious but kind of, um, fragrant lunches. Sometimes you had to be a good friend to sit with Amy at lunch. But that wasn't it.

"I'm sick of Too Tall," Amy said.

"What?" I asked. "You said he was the greatest."

"Well," Amy said, "I must have meant the greatest show-off and bully in the world. I'm really sorry about what he did at your practice the other day."

"Don't worry about that," I told her. "Actually, it turned out all right for the Rangers. Everybody felt so mad about what Too Tall did to Alex that we practiced great after that." I paused. "What about Michael?" I asked.

Amy rolled her eyes. "It's like he's been taken over by aliens or something! Look at him!"

Over at the Orioles' table, half the kids were squeezing their hands in their armpits to make loud noises. The other half were turning their eyelids inside out and moaning like monsters. Michael was trying to do both. And he and Too Tall Henry had matching ketchup stains on the front of their shirts.

"Maybe he'll go back to being his normal self during soccer season," Amy said.

"It could be worse, I guess," I told her. I was trying to look on the bright side. "I have really nice kids on a really terrible team. You have really obnoxious kids on a really good team. At least neither one of us has to play with really obnoxious kids on a really terrible team."

Amy and I were still laughing about that when we heard Mr. Becker's voice across the room. "Miiiiister Grassi, Miiiiister Henry, Miiiiiss Petrie," he was saying. "That's it. Let's go pay a visit to Mrs. Morton's office, right now."

Oh, no. The principal, I thought.

"Poor Michael," said Amy.

Just then a loud crashing noise came from the other side of the cafeteria. Amy and I looked over in time to see Josh Ramos, Adam Fingerhut, and Alex Slavik all getting up off the floor. Somehow all three of them had managed to tip over their chairs at the same time. They all stood there rubbing their heads and trying to act as if it didn't hurt.

Then they all leaned over together to pick up their chairs and—*bam!*—they crashed heads again. So they stood there again, blaming each other and acting brave while they all muttered "Ouch!" and "Oooh!" under their breath.

Amy and I cracked up.

Earlier that week I had stayed after. I'd told Ms. Kellam I needed extra help with multiplying in two columns. Really, though, I hadn't wanted to walk with Amy and Michael and hear all about the Orioles. But on Wednesday afternoon I met Amy at the door and we walked together.

"Good luck this evening," I told her as we reached the Powells' driveway.

"Good luck to the Rangers," Amy said.

"Thanks!" I called out as she headed to her front door. As I walked away I thought of Adam, Josh, and Alex massaging their heads in the cafeteria and said to myself, *We need it!*

Chapter 7

The day had started off cloudy, but at five-thirty Wednesday afternoon it was bright and warm. Lots of people had turned out for the Rangers-Orioles game. There were moms and dads, little brothers and sisters, even a few dogs. Some families even brought picnics and ate in the park before game time. I had eaten early to stay light on my feet for the game. Also, my stomach was doing these funny flip-flops.

The recreation department had been working to make the field look more like a real baseball diamond. They had put a big metal cage behind home plate to stop out-of-control balls. There were benches for each team, one between home plate and first base, the other between third base and home plate. A few feet behind the benches were bleachers for the spectators.

I helped Mom unload the equipment—bats, balls, and helmets—from the trunk of the car as the players gathered. Danny West was one of the first to come. He had on a brand-new pair of sneakers.

As soon as Brenda arrived she went from picnic to picnic, looking for leftovers. Matt and Lucy came together, with Lucy cartwheeling her way across the field. Alex came wearing Yin's good-luck charm and carrying Danny's glove, with Josh's cloth hanging from his back pocket. He must have eaten Brenda's lollipop.

Julie was the last Ranger to arrive. "It's very hard to match the rest of an outfit to this T-shirt," she explained. She was wearing blue jeans, just like everyone else. But she had replaced her white shoelaces with green ones, to match our team T-shirt.

The Rangers gathered in a huddle, and Mom gave a pep talk. "Remember," she

said, "each one of you is like a flower. One may be shorter, one may be taller, one may have a different smell—"

"Yeah, pee-yew!" Matt said, shoving Lucy.

"But each one of these flowers is important in the garden." Mom ended her little speech with a big, satisfied-looking smile.

"Huh?" Mitchell said.

"Never mind," I told everybody. "She's kind of crazy about flowers. What she means is that a team needs everybody."

We all put our hands one on top of the other in a big pile and shouted, "Go, Rangers! Go, Rangers! Go, go, go!" Then we threw our hands up in the air.

Let's Go Rangers!!

It was time to play the Orioles.

The Rangers were up first. Adam stepped to the plate and knocked the ball into center field, where the Orioles' fielder couldn't get to it in time. He made it all the way to second base. Matt went next and got a single. The knots in my stomach began to dissolve. At least it wasn't a disaster.

We followed with a few strikeouts, but more base hits. "All right, everybody, come way in," Coach Popple yelled when Yin stepped up to the plate.

Bang! was the noise of Yin's bat meeting the ball and launching it way out over the Orioles' heads. Yin drove in our first three runs.

Soon the score was Rangers 4, Orioles 0. Of course, the Orioles hadn't had a chance to bat yet, but it still sounded great.

Alex was the last of the Rangers to bat. Lucy, Matt, and Adam all patted him on the shoulder as he stepped up to the plate.

Alex swung and got a nice piece of the ball. With a *plock,* it zoomed across the field. Alex ran toward first base—and Josh Ramos's hundred-pound shaggy black Newfoundland dog ran after him. Maybe he recognized the little pink piece of blankie that was fluttering in the breeze as Alex ran.

The dog was a lot faster than Alex, and he caught up with him about five feet in front of first base, where he tackled him and started licking him like crazy. But even flat on his back, Alex was determined. He stretched for first base, but he couldn't quite reach it. The Orioles' first baseman stepped on the bag, and the umpire shouted, "He's out!"

Chapter
8

The Rangers and the Orioles traded places, and the coaches had a conference on the pitcher's mound. Nobody had ever seen a dog make an out before. But I guess they decided it would be too much trouble to do the play over—or maybe they worried that Alex would be tackled again. So the only thing that happened was that Josh's dog got ejected from the game, and from the park . . . for the entire season.

"The kid's a jinx!" Josh said to me as we picked up our gloves.

"Whatsa matter, Josh?" teased Adam. "He won't give your blankie back?" Josh lunged for him, but Adam was too quick.

50

As the game went on, it looked as if Josh might be right. The Orioles hit ball after ball after ball. And the Rangers missed every single one. Balls went over our gloves, under our gloves, through our legs, everywhere but into our gloves. I had to keep reminding myself that there was one problem with Josh's jinx theory. The Rangers had been bad before Alex was ever on the team.

At the end of the first inning the score was Orioles 7, Rangers 4.

The second inning was even worse. Danny, Yin, and Brenda all turned out to be afraid of dogs. Danny and Yin both hit the ball, but they didn't make it to first. They were too afraid a dog would tackle them, too. Brenda wouldn't even bat. Alex struck out.

Then when the Orioles were up at bat, it was a repeat of the first inning, except that we did get one out. Amy, the lefty, was up, and she hit the ball into right field. Most people are right-handed, and right-handed people almost never hit the ball into right field. So until Amy was up, nobody noticed Mitchell lying in right field, not moving.

When Mitchell didn't even move for

Amy's ball, everyone rushed over to see what had happened.

Mitchell was flat on his back, arms over his head, fast asleep in right field—with the ball tucked into his glove. And he was snoring.

At the end of the second inning, the score was Orioles 10, Rangers 6.

The Rangers were very quiet during the snack break between the second and third innings.

"That's it," Josh finally said. "We're doomed to last place."

"Maybe," Julie said. "But at least we look nice. Look how dirty the Orioles' T-shirts are. I bet those stains won't come out."

"Are you going to eat your fruit roll?" Brenda asked Alex, who was sitting at the end of our bench, scuffing his shoes back and forth in the dust.

"Yo, dudes!" a voice boomed. *Oh, no,* I thought. Just what we didn't need—a visit from Too Tall Henry. Right behind him were a few other Orioles, including Michael.

"Hey," Too Tall said, "I gotta go right after the game. So I just thought I'd come over now to wish you better luck next time. I mean, you can't lose 'em all." He scratched his big head, as if he was thinking about something. "Or maybe you guys *can* lose 'em all."

"Huh huh huh," laughed his buddies.

The whole time Too Tall was talking, Alex just kept his head down and went on swinging his feet.

But Yin jumped up from the bench, throwing her fruit roll down on the ground. Brenda looked pretty sad about that, but she didn't move.

"Hey!" Yin said. "You get lost! Rangers win! Orioles lose! Orioles stink!" Baseball was improving Yin's English fast.

"Henry!" a grown-up voice called from across the field. "Grassi! MacKenzie! Jordan! *Here! Now!*"

Coach Popple did not sound happy. Too Tall and his buddies moved fast to get back to their side of the field.

But Too Tall had already made a big mistake. Now the Rangers were mad. Really mad!

"Who he thinks he is?" said Yin. "Rangers gonna win!"

"Yeah," said Lucy, smiling. "Rangers gonna win!" She grabbed Matt's hand and began swinging it, shouting, "Rangers gonna win! Rangers gonna win!"

Soon we were all shouting, "Rangers gonna win! Rangers gonna win!" Even Josh and Adam, who refused to hold hands, were shouting.

Across the field, we could see Coach Popple talking angrily to Too Tall and the rest of his gang.

When the third inning began and we Rangers stepped up to the plate one by one, we were steamed.

Crack! Josh rocketed the ball for a double.

Thwack! Adam doubled, driving Josh home.

Smack! Lucy hit a single, followed— *whack!*—by another single from Matt.

Plock! Even Brenda bunted her way to first base.

The bases were loaded when Yin stepped up, and—*ker-whack!* She pounded the ball for a grand slam—four more runs!

When the last Ranger had batted, the score was Rangers 14, Orioles 10. We cheered and yelled as we took our positions in the field.

Chapter 9

Unfortunately, being mad did not help the Rangers too much with our fielding.

One by one, the Orioles hit the ball past us. We must have made them nervous, though. No one was hitting the ball too far.

Still, one base at a time, we watched the score change: 14–10, then 14–11, then 14–12. Amy scored the run that made it 14–13. She looked over at me and shrugged. But I didn't blame her. She was an Oriole, after all.

There were three runners on base when Too Tall Henry, hitting last in the Orioles' batting order, came to the plate. The field was so quiet, you could almost hear the sound of the grass growing. If Too Tall could drive in at least two runs, the Orioles would win the game. If not, the Rangers would win everything. It would be a major upset—especially for Too Tall Henry.

Too Tall stepped up to the plate. He stood at home plate and pounded the end of the bat into the dust. Then he raised his hand to his batting helmet and touched the bill one, two, three times.

At last Too Tall was ready. He lifted the bat and swung with all his power.

He hit a high fly. The ball went up, up, up. Then it began to come down, down, down, headed straight for Alex Slavik in center field.

IT'S A

Alex's eyes grew wide with terror. He turned and ran forward, then changed his mind and ran back. He was about to change his mind one more time when he tripped over his own enormous feet.

As the entire crowd groaned, Alex landed flat as a pancake on the field just as the ball came down.

Smack! The ball fell straight into Alex's wide-open glove.

"I got it!" he yelled. "I got it! I got it!" He threw the ball wildly into the air. It came down in the neighborhood of second base, where Josh Ramos snagged it and tagged out Chris MacKenzie. Josh fired the ball to Matt at home plate, who handed the ball to Michael Grassi as he headed in from third.

Michael was so confused, he took it.

"Out! Out! Out!" called the umpire.

It was the triple play of my dreams, only better.

Josh and Adam grabbed Alex and lifted him onto their shoulders. Well, actually, they dropped him, and he banged his ankle so hard we thought maybe it was broken. But it wasn't.

Lucy and Matt did handstands across the field.

"Watch out for the flowers!" Mom yelled. But even she grabbed Brenda and Mitch and Yin and me in a great big hug and jumped up and down.

In the middle of the celebration, the Orioles came over to shake hands and congratulate us.

Too Tall barely shook hands. "I guess he's in a big hurry because he has to go someplace soon," Julie said with a grin.

When Michael came over, he shook my hand, but he wouldn't look at me.

"Congratulations," Amy said as she came up. "I'm sorry about Michael."

"Me too," I said. "But soccer season will be here sooner or later."

Amy looked happy about that.

"All right, Rangers," Mom said when things had quieted down. "What about a little celebration?"

"Yaaaay!" we all shouted.

"Pizza!" Brenda yelled.

"Yaaaay!" we said.

"And ice cream!" she added.

"Yaaaay!" we cried.

"And cake!" she shouted.

"I think I'm gonna be sick," Mitchell Rubin said.

Mom laughed. "Let's save something for our next victory, Brenda," she suggested.

Everybody liked the sound of that. And we all followed Yin off the field as she led the way, shouting, "Rangers number one! Rangers number one! Rangers number one!"

And the Rangers *were* number one—for the moment, at least. . . .

ASPHODEL PUBLIC LIBRARY
WESTWOOD, ONT. K0L 3B0

THE LEFTOVERS #2: CATCH FLIES!

by Tristan Howard

Okay, so the Rangers are the worst team in the league. All they need is a little practice, right? But how can they practice when Lucy and Matt can't stop fighting?

COMING IN JUNE!

L01095